T0381137

THE ADVENTURES OF JUNETEENA FREEMAN

"CROWN"

DISCOVER A NEW JUNETEENTH SUPERHERO WHO GAINS POWERS BY KNOWING HER HISTORY OF HER ANCESTORS

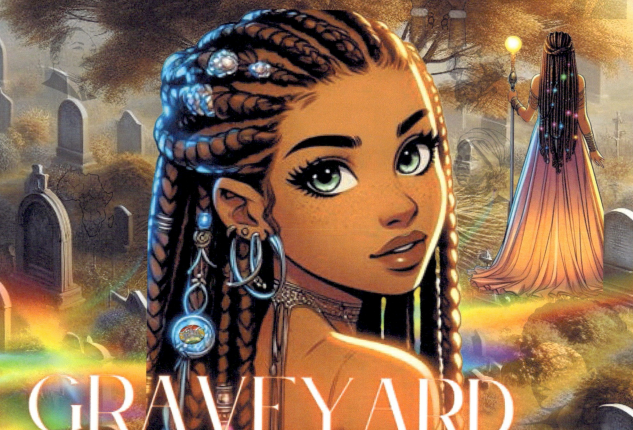

GRAVEYARD IN THE ATTIC

CREATED BY DR. TUCKER-JOHNSON
WRITTEN BY DR. PHYLLIS TUCKER-WICKS

HOW IT ALL BEGAN

JUNETEENA WAS A BEAUTIFUL LITTLE GIRL WHO LOVED READING BOOKS. SHE HAD LONGED TO GET A HOLD OF THE BOOKS HER MOTHER KEPT IN THE ATTIC BUT MOM TOLD JUNETEENA SHE COULD NOT READ THESE BOOKS UNTIL SHE WAS OF AGE. BUT WHAT AGE WOULD THIS BE JUNETEENA ALWAYS WONDERED.

WRITTEN BY: DR. TUCKER-WICKS

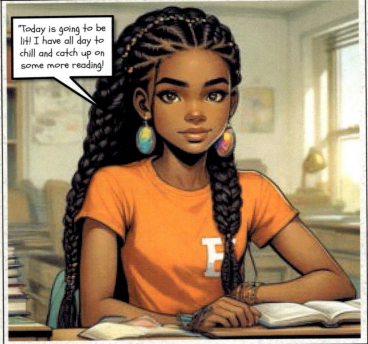

"Today is going to be lit! I have all day to chill and catch up on some more reading!"

SHE STARTED READING VERY YOUNG BUT NEVER FOUND THE INFORMATION THAT WOULD CHANGE HER LIFE.

WHEN JUNETEENA BECAME 13, SHE HAD THE SAME INSTINCTS AS ANY TEENAGER.

IT'S CALLED BEING NOSY. SHE KNEW MOM WAS A HOARDER AND JUNETEENA BECAME TIRED OF ALWAYS ASKING QUESTIONS ABOUT THE BOOKS IN THE ATTIC. IT SEEMED LIKE EVERY YEAR WOULD GO BY AND JUNETEENA WOULD ASK HER MOM ABOUT THE BOOKS BUT HER MOTHER WOULD ALWAYS ANSWER BY SAYING, "WHEN YOU BECOME OF AGE". HER MOM WAS NEVER TELLING HER WHAT THIS AGE WAS SO JUNETEENA WENT SNOOPING AROUND AND FOUND HER WAY TO THE ATTIC....

BUT COULDN'T GET THE DOOR UNLOCKED.

JUNETEENA FREEMAN WAS NOW 13 YEARS OLD. SHE DIDN'T KNOW MUCH ABOUT HERSELF OTHER THAN ALL THE STORIES HER SINGLE MOTHER WOULD TELL HER ABOUT THE TIME HER GREAT-GREAT GRANDPARENTS THAT WERE KILLED IN THE TULU MASSACRE THAT TOOK PLACE IN 1921.

SHE KNEW THAT SHE WAS NAMED JUNE IN THEIR MEMORY AND HER MOM FELT IT WAS HER RESPONSIBILITY TO DISCOVER WHO SHE REALLY WAS ON HER OWN.

3

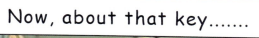

Now, about that key.......

Juneteena! I know you're looking for the key to the attic. Don't waste your time. You won't find it dear! You can get the books when you become of age.

Juneteena searched the Kitchen, Her Mother's Bedroom, and even in the study...

It's useless. Mother has hidden both the key to the Attic and to my family history. Both are on LOCK.

I need a Hobby

You already have hobbies dear!

Everywhere Juneteena looked, the attic key was nowhere to be found.

4

IT SEEMED LIKE EVERY TIME SHE READ A BLACK HISTORY BOOK, SHE BECAME EMOTIONAL

Why does this hurt so badly?

MEANWHILE....

STRANGE THINGS STARTED HAPPENING THAT JUNETEENA COULDN'T EXPLAIN!

JUNETEENA ALSO WOULD HAVE OUTBURST OF ANGER. #BIGMAD

*!#@

...AND SHE STARTED SINGING OLD NEGRO SPIRITUALS THAT SHE HAD NEVER KNOWN AND DIDN'T KNOW WHY///

"Take Me To The River..

SHE WOULD ALSO MEDITATE FROM TIME TO TIME.........AND DIDN'T KNOW WHY...

5

WHEN NIGHTFALL CAME, SHE WOULD ALWAYS DREAM OF BEING A QUEEN, BUT SHE DIDN'T KNOW WHY.

.....AND IT DIDNT END THERE!

THE NEXT DAY...
JUNETEENA WAS SINGING IN HER MICROPHONE AND SHE HEARD ANOTHER VOICE SINGING WITH HER. SHE NOTICED IT WAS COMING FROM THE ATTIC.

JUNETEENA WANTED DESPERATELY TO KNOW WHERE THE VOICE WAS COMING FROM SO SHE FOLLOWED THE VOICE AND IT LED HER STRAIGHT TO THE ATTIC!

"WHAT IS HAPPENING? .....MOM?."

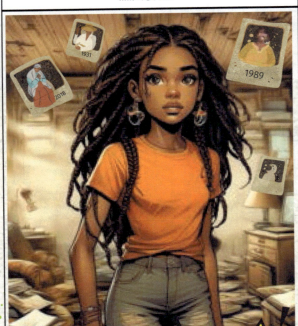

AND THERE IT WAS...
A FLOATING PICTURE OF GRANDMOTHER MARETHA, WHO WAS FONDLY KNOWN AS GRANDMOTHER RITA. THE BEAUTIFUL PICTURE WAS JUST FLOATING IN AIR

BUT THAT IS NOT ALL JUNETEENA SAW......

WHAT IN THE WORLD!!

OMG!

"SOMETHING ABOUT THIS FAMILIAR.... ALMOST NOSTALGIC."

"Shes Here"

"Why She look crazy?"

"Shes so beautiful"

"Come Closer"

"...and powerful too!"

"Time To Go! Our attic is ... HAUNTED!!"

AT FIRST, JUNETEENA WAS STUNNED, BUT THEN SHE FELT WARMTH AND LOVE. AS SOON AS SHE RELAXED,

A BEAUTIFUL WOMAN APPEARED IN THE LIGHT, & BEGAN TO SPEAK TO HER.

"......GRANDMA RITA?"

AS GRANDMA RITA WELCOMED JUNETEENA, SHE QUICKLY TOLD HER THAT THERE WAS MUCH TO LEARN AND THAT JUNETEENA HAD A VERY SPECIAL DESTINY AHEAD.

BUT FIRST......

This is UNBELIEVABLE But how...

13

Suddenly, lightning struck! Then, out of the darkness, voices of her Ancestors started to speak and materialize before her very eyes........

One by One, members of her blood line appeared to greet this "powerful one,"

There was Uncle Peter, a Protector during the Trans-Atlantic Slave Trade.

Aunt Melshonda, a Revolutionist & Civil Rights Activist in the Historic Black Panther Party

I am your Uncle Arnold. My life was cut short in the Elaine Massacre.

Juneteena stood in amazement as she listened intentfully to each of her Ancestor's stories and experiences.

Juneteena was AMAZED as others emerged to introduce themselves..

She learned that through "All Time," her bloodline had lived, experienced, and prevailed...

"I'm Yvonne andI was sold on a slave block, never to reunite in life with my family..."

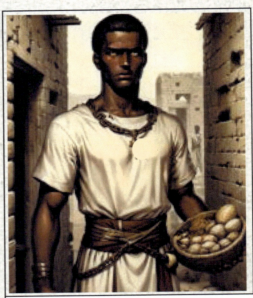

..and I was just a Sinner. I disobeyed the Laws of The Creator...repeatedly!

Only if we would obey the laws of the Creator... I'm your Aunt Rose. I call you through the petals. I died during the Civil Rights. movement.

..and there was even MORE to learn as her Ancestors appeared...

Young and Old, one by one, her family tree was becoming crystal clear!

Hey JUNETEENA!! I'm yo cousin Hattie. I was marching for Justice & got beat! Where's yo uncle Clyde?

HUH?!

"Here I am right here Hattie Mae. Is this the descendant all y'all been talking about who 'pose to have some super powers? We done been down here a long time. The only superpower she needs is this grass. This some good weed!"

"Clyde, you old skeezer! You done been in the ground TOO LONG! You gone scare the girl. How you doing baby girl?"

Then, Papa Abraham came forth, the Patriach of our family!

I AM ABRAHAM, YOUR OLDEST ELDER. THROUGH MY OBEDIENCE TO OUR CREATOR, OUR BRANCHES GREW.

FROM THE ANCIENT TRIBES OF AFRICA

THROUGH THE ATROCITIES OF HUMANKIND...

OUR ROOTS SPREAD AND GREW.

We are like Trees the ROOT of all mankind.

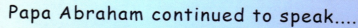

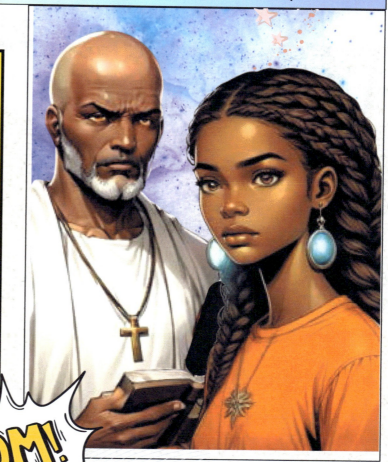

"You are powerful, Juneteena." And it is from these roots that your strength and source of power derive from.

From the sands of the Serengeti through the Journey to the New World, you carry the Power of all your Ancestors- Linked to the Most High, that have come Before YOU."

BOOM!

Your Power Runs From, To, & Through the Ancestors.

Juneteena now begun to understand. She started remembering stories she had read about and the black experiences of people that she felt connected to. People whom she had never met!

Juneteena decided to ask the beautiful woman,, Grandma Rita, who are all these people?

Grandma Rita started to tell Juneteena more about the importance of understanding "Who We Are." She also told Juneteena to listen with her heart, mind, & spirit so she could hear the voices of her Ancestors.

"We are your Ancestors, child. We have called you through the light so that you may know Yourself, Your Strength, & Your Power!"

Suddenly, an overwhelming sadness came over Juneteena. From all the Ancestors who had come forward to greet her, her heart aches immensely still............

"I'm so confused! I don't understand.
Did Mama know about this?
What happened to my daddy?
Where is MY DADDY?"

SHHH!

Hey now, Juneteena. Everything is going to be OK! I'm your Uncle Philip. I promise you--you will see your Dad again. Your daddy isn't ready to see you yet, and don'tbe mad at your Mom."

OK, But I'm still sad about that and confused. Why are you all here?...in Mom's Attic?"

21

Juneteena is so confused. Is she still in her attic..or is she standing in a graveyard? She wonders if she has lost her mind! Thunder Strikes! The Oak tree starts to glow, and then a beautiful crown appears before her very eyes.

Then "IT" spoke....

The Crown told the history she had already known about Juneteenth. What she did not know, was there would be a twist in the Juneteenth story.

Juneteenth commemorates an effective end of slavery in the United States, and soon, there would be Queens to arise as "Miss Juneteenth" to create the legend, that anyone who wears the crown, would receive super-powers.

from those who have experienced hatred and abuse in a movement called civil rights. These powers would lie in the crown of the person who successfully opened the door of the graveyard in the attic.

OMG

Whoa! Well look at that!

Just then, Juneteena began to see flashes of all of her ancestors before her eyes emerging from the Book of Time.

22

Just then, Juneteena began to see flashes of all of her ancestors before her eyes...emerging from the Book of Time.

"You Are THE Miss Juneteenth"

The Power of the Crown Begin to Speak Directly to Juneteena, herself:

All of your ancestors that had been killed in civil injustices around the world will awaken when you reconnect the crown to your head. Your hair serve as an antenna to the spiritual world. The Infinite Divine.

You are chosen by God. Because of your diligence in seeking to find who you really are, you will be rewarded by granting access to the powers inside of you. The cries of your ancestors produces the sound of the frequency that illuminates your crown.

Whatever injustice you see on the outside, is the injustice done to your ancestors. Where there is injustice, there will be CROWN.

YOU, JUNETEENA, ARE CROWN!

24

May 26, 1637 Pequot Massacre

Nov. 29, 1864: Sand Creek Massacre

Sept. 19, 1868: Camilla Massacre

July 30, 1866 New Orleans Massacre

Sept. 28, 1868: Opelousas Massacre

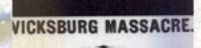

VICKSBURG MASSACRE.

Now Transpires that One Hundred a Fifty Negroes were Slaughtered.

DEC. 7, 1874 Vicksburg Massacre

Sept. 4, 1875 Clinton Mississippi Massacre

Nov. 3, 1883 Danville Riot Massacre

Mar 17, 1886: Carroll County Courthouse Massacre

Nov 23,1887:Thibodaux Massacre

Dec. 29, 1890: Wounded Knee Massacre

25

You will be transferred into the crown you wear with ALL POWER. You CAN NOT and WILL NOT be defeated. You will call up the ancestors who have gone through the injustices that will appear to you in real time and before it happens, you will rewrite history!

In this moment, Juneteena knew her purpose and her power. She was the "Chosen" one. She donned her crown and the power of all of her ancestors filled her spirit and ......

YOU ARE JUNETEENA FREEMAN. YOU ARE THE POWER OF 3! CONNECT YOUR CROWN TO YOUR ONENESS & THE THREE BECOME ME.

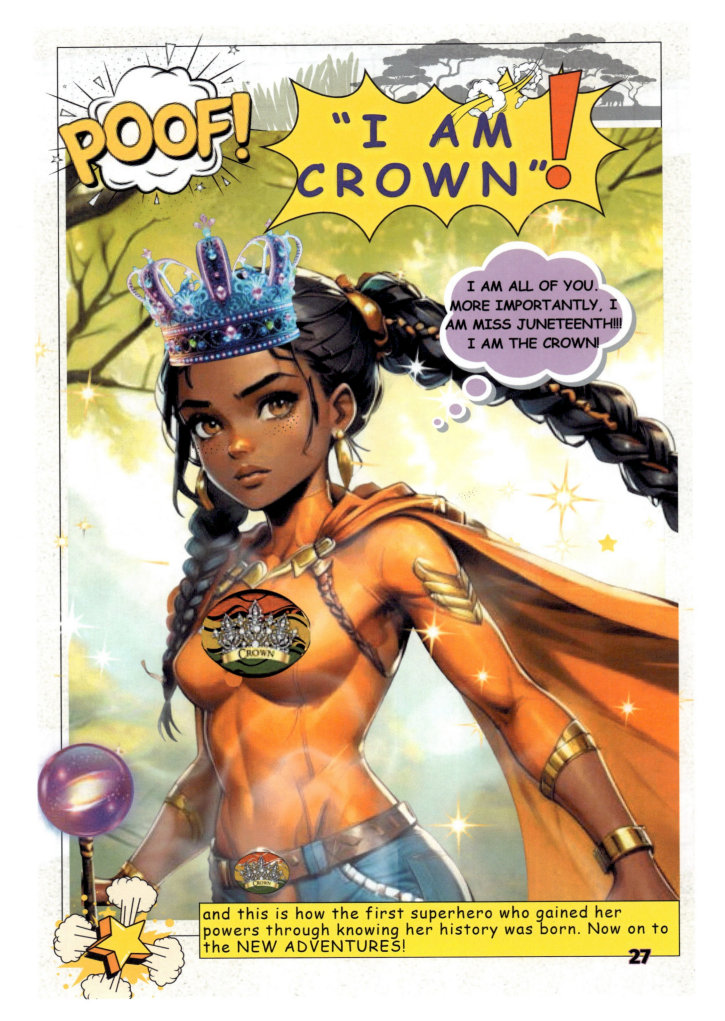

DR. PHYLLIS TUCKER-WICKS
Biography Highlights:

- Retired Language Arts School teacher of 45 years (Sligh, Stewart, Madison & Young)
- Adjunct Professor At Hillsborough Community College
- Reader Adviser of Dissertations at Nova Southeastern University
- Former Instructor at Southwest Florida College
- Former Instructor at the University Of Phoenix
- Adjunct professor at the University Of Tampa
- Instructor at Hillsborough Community College
- Miss Black Florida & Miss Black America "82"
- Key to the city of Daytona Bch. Fl. "82"
- Former Tampa Bay Buccaneer cheerleader, "82"
- Role model ambassador for Little Rock Ark presented by Governor Bill Clinton "82"
- Who's Who Among Americas Teachers "95 & 96",& "02"
- Eddie Award Nominee '93'
- Teacher Of The Month '96'
- Author of a school's philosophy "97"
- Ida S. Baker Award/Distinguished Minority Educator, "2003"
- Unsung Hero Dr. Martin Jr. award "03"
- Television Talk Show Host 2001-2009
- Martin Luther King Jr. award "2001"
- Educator Of the Year...University Of Phoenix "2009"
- Black Diamond Award Educator Of The Year "2009*
- Business owner....Bles'd Productions since "2005"
- Top five Finalist for the Oprah Winfrey Network...Your Own Show 2011
- Put together the framework for the Juneteenth curriculum
- Author of three books and has her first comic book of the upcoming introduction of our Juneteenth superhero to be released by June 14, 2024

DR. PHILETHA TUCKER-JOHNSON
Biography Highlights:

Dr. Tucker-Johnson has a Bachelor's degree in English Education, a Master's in Instruction and Curriculum, and Doctorate in Organizational Leadership with a specialty in cultural diversity. She is F.C.C. licensed and is the President of The Tampa Bay Juneteenth Coalition. Other Professional highlights of her life include:

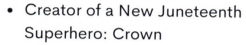

- Creator of a New Juneteenth Superhero: Crown
- Miss Juneteenth USA, Vice President
- Florida State Executive Director for the National Miss Juneteenth USA Scholarship Pageant pipeline.
- National Juneteenth Ambassadors, Founder | President
- Legacy Heirs Juneteenth Podcast
- Former Miss Homecoming of Bethune-Cookman College
- Former Miss Daytona Beach Florida
- Former Tampa Bay Buccaneer Cheerleader
- Recipient of the key to the city of Daytona Beach Florida
- Listed as Who's Who among America's teachers Eddie Award
- Nominee Ida S. Baker Award
- Distinguished Minority Educator nominee
- Recipient of the Unsung Hero Dr. Martin Luther King Jr. Award,
- Former Television Talk Show Host, 2003

Order this book online at www.trafford.com
or email orders@trafford.com

Most Trafford titles are also available at major online book retailers.

 www.trafford.com

North America & international
toll-free: 844 688 6899 (USA & Canada)
fax: 812 355 4082

Our mission is to efficiently provide the world's finest, most comprehensive book publishing service, enabling every author to experience success. To find out how to publish your book, your way, and have it available worldwide, visit us online at www.trafford.com

Because of the dynamic nature of the Internet, any web addresses or links contained in this book may have changed since publication and may no longer be valid. The views expressed in this work are solely those of the author and do not necessarily reflect the views of the publisher, and the publisher hereby disclaims any responsibility for them.

Any people depicted in stock imagery provided by Getty Images are models, and such images are being used for illustrative purposes only.
Certain stock imagery © Getty Images.

ISBN: 978-1-6987-1738-8 (sc)
        978-1-6987-1739-5 (e)

Library of Congress Control Number: 2024916119

Print information available on the last page.

Trafford rev. 07/26/2024